Wigan, Pies And Rugby
Pie Eater Kev

All poems copyright © Kevin Fitzpatrick 2022
All images and photographs created by Kevin Fitzpatrick unless otherwise stated.

About The Author

Kev Fitzpatrick
@PieEaterKev

Wiganer exiled in Wakefield 🏵 Single Dad of two 💀 👻 School science tech 🏉 Love Rugby League 🍒 ⚪ ✏️ writing poems 🎸 playing guitar & quaffing fine ales 🍺

Photograph of a Central Park, Wigan from www.cherryandwhite.co.uk, photographer unknown.

Acknowledgements

I would like to say thank you to all the people who have continued to encourage me to write and publish my poems. A special mention goes out to The Cherry and White fanzine and The Wigan MS Society. Some of these poems first saw the light of day in publications they produced.

As always a big thank you to my friend Lou for taking the time to proof read this collection. Not only did she correct my spelling and grammar but she also pointed out that words spoken in a Wigan accent don't necessarily rhyme when spoken in normal English.

It's great to have a tater pie,
On such pies I have grown.
But it's better with some pea wet,
Man can't live on pie alone.

Contents

Wigan Kebabs	15
Don't Forget The Pies	16
The Battle Of Wigan Lane	18
And All Because The Lady Loves Pie	20
The Other White Horse Final	22
What Exactly Is A Flittin?	23
Ten Tries	24
Mum Knows Best	25
Trick Or Treat?	26
I Have A Dream	27
Bedsheet O'er My Head	28
Nellie Bispham's Gonna Get Ya	29
Puis (Peesh) Aubert	30
Down At The Wigan Roller Rink	31
Treat For Santa	32
Ten Yards Short	33
Half A Lane Too Thin	34
From Blue Stripes To Cherry Hoops	35
River Caves Virgin	36
The Man With The Shiny Shoe	37
A View From A Bridge	38
Pie And Cloddin	39
Challenge Cup Memories	40
Pie Crusts	41
Pie And Stout	42
Three Miles Underground	43
Star Wars Comes To Wigan	44
Stamp On His Head, He Bleeds	46
Grandma Sharkey's Secret	47
The Hand Of G.O'D.	48
Humble Pie	49
Super Kel	50
Blue Monday	51
Rugby League Family	52
Polite Applause And Forced Smiles	53
Over To Our North Of England Correspondent	54
Unbelievable	55
Central Park Players	56
Banished To Leigh	58
The Impossible	59
Wigan : 1 Town, 2 Teams, 3 Trophies	60
Curse Of The Wigan Shirts	61
Blake Green	62
No Pies Are Left In This Vehicle Overnight	63
Three Stars	64

Four Gold Stars	65
Russian Spies	66
Billy	67
Pies, Mints And Rock n Roll	68
Confiscated Pies	69
Topless Pies	70
The Wrong Pies	71
Mint Ball Addict	72
Wagin Bere Fetsvial Peom	73
There's Only One True Derby Game	74
Heinz Roulette	75
Deconstructed Pie With Pea Jus	76
Beer And Tear Stains	77
Ever Wondered How Santa…	78
Turkeys Aren't Nervous In Wigan…	79
I Only Have Pies For You	80
We Make Pies Not War	81
Who Needs Crusts?	82
Pie Eyed	83
New Kit Revealed	84
A New Anthem For England	85
Wot No Pie?	86
Suck On An Uncle Joe	87
Dom Manfredi	88
Soggy	89
Wigan Yorkshire Dwarves	90
Have The Leythers Gone All Soft?	92
Super Shiny Shoe	93
Enjoy A Pie Barm…	94
Martial Arts Of Wigan	96
Who Would Be A Referee?	97
Wigan Budgie Smugglers	98
Joe Daniels	99
Scholeshenge	100
Just A Bus Stop In Wigan	101
British Pie Week	102
4th Of July	103
Trouble Down At Wigan Zoo	104
Turkey Dinner Incident	105
Sheep Stops Play	106
Pie-rish	107
I Don't Wanna Talk About It	108
Dr Kathleen Drew Baker	110
There's Always Time For Pie	111
Keeping The Faith	112
A Season To Forget	113
Smuggling Pies	114
Wigan Casino	115
A Pie A Day	116

Introduction

In 15BC, Roman poet Sextus Aurelius Propertius wrote "Absence makes the heart grow fonder". This is certainly true. I'm sure many of my fellow Wiganers take for granted meeting up regularly with friends and family and going down to the Pie Dome, grabbing a Galloway's pie en route and enjoying a bag of Uncle Joe's mint balls at half time. These days I only get over occasionally to see my family and as for following my rugby team, I see them play more in Yorkshire than at home these days.

I really feel a sense of belonging when I'm over in Wigan. It's often a wrench to leave and sometimes I wish I could stay. Unfortunately my current circumstances mean that a permanent return isn't possible, but it doesn't stop me writing about the place. Wigan, Pies and Rugby is a collection of poems that celebrate my home town. They include childhood memories, local history as well as many of the pie and rugby related poems I have written over the years. Be you a Wiganer or not, I hope you enjoy the book.

Happy reading

Pie Eater Kev August 2022

Wigan Kebabs

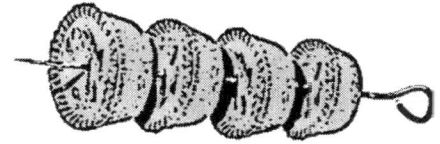

Some folk like eating caviar,
And some the legs of frogs.
While others love their truffles
And go foraging with hogs.
But in a certain town
They're considered second rate.
Instead folk head to pie shops,
Where they have to queue and wait.
For pies all stuck on skewers,
Or placed inside a butty.
They simply cannot get enough,
Most people think they're nutty.
But if you're feeling peckish
Why not hail yourself a cab,
And get yourself to Wigan
For a Wigan Pie Kebab.

This poem is dedicated to my Auntie Pat who loves a pie barm
(a Wigan doner kebab).

Don't Forget The Pies

It's Wigan v Saints at Wembley, a chance to win the cup,
But in the Wigan changing room, it's clear that something's up.
Old Keith the Wigan kit man, in charge of all supplies,
Has turned a whiter shade of pale, "I've forgot to pack the pies!"

Thus starts a big commotion, grown men all start to cry.
Without their secret weapon, they'll never score a try.
The coach is far from happy, at Keith he starts to fume.
Keith decides to grab his phone, and swiftly leaves the room.

So with their bellies rumbling, and The Saints all full of scouse,
They walk onto the hallowed turf, and a noisy packed full house.
Wigan are truly awful, they miss tackles and knock on,
The Saints are up by 30 points, the chance of winning gone.

But just before the half time break, help's not too far away.
A Wigan pie van at great speed, turns onto Wembley Way.
The Wigan lads walk off the pitch, they're feeling sad and glum,
But standing there is smiling Keith, "Cheer up lads - pies have come!"

The players' faces light up, they can't believe their eyes,
For waiting for them on a tray, the finest Wigan pies.
The forwards eat the steak ones, the backs have meat 'n' tater,
No time to pour on pea wet, they'll have to have that later.

The Wigan lads now full of pie, run out with smile on face.
The forwards feel much stronger, and the backs are full of pace.
The forwards are fantastic, players falling off their backs.
The Saints they have no answer, to the barrage of attacks.

The ball is passed along the line, the backs are running hot.
The mighty Saints are powerless, their defence has gone to pot.
The Wigan fans go crazy, a sea of flag and scarf,
Wigan racking up the points, Saints can't get out their half.

And so the final hooter blows, The Challenge Cup is won.
A story that will now be passed, from father down to son.
Old Keith runs over, jug in hand, and in the cup does pour
Not champagne but pea wet, he'd promised them before.

So the moral of this story, should come as no surprise,
If Wigan get to Wembley, please don't forget the pies!

Written after the death of Keith Mills, a long serving member of the back room staff. He performed most roles at the club from physio to water carrier. No doubt he would've been in charge of the pies.

The Battle of Wigan Lane

You may have passed a monument that stands on Wigan Lane.
Don't know what it's all about? Well please let me explain.
The year is 1651, the time of civil war,
A time of gruesome battles, of blood and guts and gore.
Our tale concerns two local lads, from Knowsley and from Leigh.
Cavaliers of great esteem, known for their loyalty.
Tom was born at Morleys Hall, in war he made his mark,
While James came from a grand estate, now a safari park.

Tom was on the Isle of Man when James came round one night,
"Get your armour packed young lad, we have to go and fight.
The King is on the up again as far as I can tell.
He's coming down from Scotland and he wants to bash Cromwell.
Join me back in Lancashire, an army we will muster.
We could 'ave some pie n peas then meet the King in Worcester."
So off they went to Lancashire, recruiting on the way,
But many men were busy and weren't coming out to play.

They all rode on to Wigan Town, to 'ave them pie n peas,
But Cromwell's men were waiting, all hiding in the trees.
They rode into a mêlée of pike, musket and cleaver.
The records state that James was hit on breast plate and on beaver*
But James still charged The Roundheads, this time with fewer men.
They could've done with Uncle Joes, but they didn't make em then.
The third charge was to be their last; they knew that they were beat.
Despite their skill and bravery, it ended in defeat.

Nursing many injuries, our James he got away,
Hiding down in Market Street to fight another day.
But Tom he didn't make it, like many he was slain,
His body lifeless in the mud, just sprawled on Wigan Lane.
And now there is a monument that marks where he did die,
He never got to eat his peas, he never had that pie.
So if you're walking down the Lane, off to the Bowling Green,
Stop off at the monument, picture the battle scene.

Recalling the Battle of Wigan Lane where Royalist forces, lead by James Stanley (7th Earl of Derby) and Sir Thomas Tyldesley, were ambushed by Cromwell's Roundheads.

*Beaver: a piece of plate armour for covering the lower part of the face and throat worn especially with an open helmet.

And All Because The Lady Loves Pie

Scene 1

A chopper hovers skilfully
Above the flats in Scholes.
A side door it slides open and
A length of rope unrolls.
A young man starts to abseil down
Onto a balconee.
All dressed in black from head to toe,
Which makes him hard to see.

He waves and signals all is well,
The rope it is untied.
He crouches down and picks the lock
And quickly slips inside.
He slowly scans around the room
And glances at the clock.
He really hasn't got much time,
A key turns in the lock.

Scene 2

She turns the key, enters her flat,
She's feeling really rough.
Her boss has give her grief all day
And now she's had enough.
Her frown it soon turns to a smile
For there before her eyes,
A calling card placed on a tray
Of meat n tater pies.

Her terrace door is still ajar,
And walking out she sees,
A rope has been tied from the rails
And down into some trees.
She stands and stares across to Town
And smiling she does note,
That on the River Douglas is
A speeding motorboat.

Written after reading that the 'Milk Tray Man' was to make a comeback. If Galloways made TV adverts...

The Other White Horse Final

In footage of the FA Cup, a white horse you can see.
It's clearing people from the pitch in 1923.
It happened too in rugby league in 1924.
The Wigan - Oldham Challenge Cup, a game set in folklore.

The players, police and horses forced the fans all back in touch.
And so it was the rugby game wasn't delayed too much.
Amidst the chaos, Wigan scored a try stranger than most.
Dodging around an in-goal horse they scored next to the post.

A try was touched down at the toes of an excited youth.
Another try was disallowed beneath a horse's hoof.
And when a winger on the side was tackled into touch,
He smashed into an infirm fan breaking the poor man's crutch.

The Pies they sealed the victory as o'er the line they ploughed.
The scorer simply disappeared enveloped by the crowd.
So Wigan won the Challenge Cup the first one of their haul,
In what has to be the most bizarre final of them all.

In 1924, over 41,000 spectators paid to see the Challenge Cup Final between Wigan and Oldham at Rochdale's Athletic Ground. Unfortunately several more found their way in without paying, resulting in the crowd spilling onto the pitch. Spectators ended up standing right up against the touchline.

What Exactly is a Flittin?

What exactly is a flittin?
I'd really like to know,
Coz mum would say I'd fell off one
When I walked through the door.
My face all dirty, caked in mud,
My clothes all ripped and splittin'.
I looked like I'd been in a fight,
Or "Just fell off a flittin."

A strange Lancashire expression that my Mum used to say after I'd been out playing.

RLIMERICKS

Ten Tries

Young Martin he played for the Pies
And caught Leeds by total surprise
He supported his side
Up the middle and wide
And ended up scoring ten tries

It's the 1992 Premiership semi-final against Leeds at Central Park and Martin Offiah pops up all over the field and ends up scoring ten tries.

Mum Know Best

Money spiders bring you wealth
If on you they do land.
But I've not won the lottery
When one's been in my hand.
If your left ear starts a burning
You've gained someone's affection.
But all it means when mine is red
Is a painful ear infection.
So I'm not a great believer
In these silly old wives tales,
But here is one from Wigan Town,
And this one never fails.
When mother used to wipe my face,
She'd use my soggy nappy,
Coz wee stopped spots apparently,
I wasn't very happy.
But during adolescence,
I reaped all the benefits,
So while my friends erupted,
My face was free from zits.

Was this common practice in 1960s Wigan or did this just happen to me? Anyway it seemed to work.

Trick or Treat?

My mum and dad were going out,
They said that they'd be late.
So I was set for a quiet night,
But I'd forgot about the date.

It was the last day in October,
Yes the night of tricks and treats.
And I'd been left without a stash
Of chews or sticky sweets.

And so the doorbell it did ring,
Lads donned in ghostly sheet.
Bit old for dressing up I thought,
They mumbled "trick or treat?"

"I haven't any treats" I said
"It'll have to be a trick."
They both gave a mischievous look,
And turned round quite quick.

With backs to me I heard them laugh,
Things about to turn quite sour,
For underneath the sheets they had
Some eggs and lots of flour.

They quickly turned and threw the lot
And gave me quite a fright,
And in an instant I had turned
A sticky shade of white.

Off they ran with me in shock,
I'd no sweets when it mattered.
They left me standing in the porch,
Not bruised but very battered.

A true story. I now make sure I'm always stocked up with sweets on Halloween.

I Have a Dream

I dream I'm in the Wigan shirt,
My name upon the back.
A favourite with the Wigan fans,
Loose forward in the pack.
I'm stepping out at Wembley,
Scoring the winning try.
I'm holding up the Challenge Cup
And celebration pie.
Parading on the open bus,
Above the engine rev,
I hear the chanting from the crowd,
"There's one Pie Eater Kev!"
The chants turn into my alarm,
I open heavy eyes.
It's time to get up, go to work,
So slowly I arise.
No playing in the Wigan shirt,
For me and many more,
It's just worn on the terraces,
Then hung behind the door.

Written after I finally got my name put on the back of my Wigan shirt.
We can all dream.

Bed Sheet O'er My Head (Halloween In Standish)

There were no costumes in the shops,
I had to make me own.
An old bed sheet or ripped tee shirt
That I had long outgrown.
And as for pumpkins, what were those?
They'd not yet come my way,
A swede had to be hollowed out,
A task that took all day.
I'd walk around, lantern in hand,
Two candle eyes alight.
But then I'd burn my fingers as
The string would soon ignite.
Yes hallowe'en you'd find me out
Amongst the walking dead.
Burns on my hand, smelling of swede,
A bed sheet o'er my head.

Memories of a typical 1970s hallowe'en on The Bleachworks Estate, Standish.

Nellie Bispham's Gonna Get Ya

When I was just a
Cub Scout small,
We would all camp
At Bispham Hall.
The ghost stories
I do recall,
Your tent mates
Would all bet ya.

To leave the tent
Around midnight,
And wander round
The wooded site,
Your heart pounding
Your face death white,
Nellie Bispham's
Gonna get ya.

And as you're starting
To relax,
A twig beneath
A footstep cracks,
You race back for
Some midnight snacks,
Next time
She may not let ya.

Memories of 4th Wigan Cub camps at Bispham Hall, Billinge, where the ghost of Nellie Bispham is said to haunt the woods.

Puig (Peesh) Aubert

There's been some sights at Central Park
But nothing can compare,
With the antics of a French full back,
His name was Peesh Aubert,

The Wigan lads and Carcassonne
Met in a winter storm.
But still despite the ice and snow,
Young Peesh was on top form.

He'd catch high balls in just one hand,
The Wigan crowd he'd stun.
Coz legend says he had a cig
Lit in the other one.

He managed to avoid the cold,
Coz when the play allowed,
He'd keep warm, sipping coffee,
Passed over from the crowd.

But all this drinking took its toll,
He found he had to go.
In the middle of the Wigan pitch,
A patch of yellow snow.

Peesh Aubert, a rugby legend
Who really left his mark.
Not only on the fans, but in
The snow at Central Park!

March 1947 and Carcassonne beat Wigan 11-8 at Central Park. Puig (pronounced Peesh) Aubert, was the greatest French Rugby League player of his generation. He earned the nickname 'pipette' a reference to his habit of smoking during a game. In 1988 he was inducted into the Rugby League Hall of Fame.

Down At The Wigan Roller Rink

On wet weekends in Wigan,
We'd often get our thrill,
Down at the Wigan Roller Rink,
In Eckersley's old mill.
We'd pass abandoned buildings,
Broken glass upon the floor,
Until we came across a queue
Of people by a door.

I still recall that sweaty smell
That we would all encounter,
As people there took off their shoes
And then approached the counter.
We'd swap our shoes for roller boots
That had seen better days,
We'd lace them up, enter the rink,
And join the skating craze.

The DJ there would always spin
The chart hits of the day,
While we would skate around the rink,
All going the same way.
But soon the rink it would be full
Of bum to floor connections,
As on the tannoy you would hear
"Stop and change directions!"

Sirens warned to leave the rink,
It's time to up the pace,
As speed skaters to sounds of rock,
Around the rink would race.
And if your skating had impressed
And caught a young girl's eye,
You'd dodge the raindrops back to town,
And treat her to a pie.

Memories of the JJB Roller Rink, Wigan in the 80s.

Treat For Santa

My dad was kind and thoughtful
On the eve of Christmas Day.
He made us leave out beer and pie,
Help Santa on his way.
And when we woke next morning
All the beer and pie were gone.
And Dad would wake with burp and smile
"Merry Christmas everyone!"

So it turns out that Santa loves a Wigan pie and a pint, who knew?

Ten Yards Short

Wigan v Leigh at Hilton Park,
Green Vigo makes a break.
He sprints on down the Wigan wing,
Then makes a huge mistake.
He thinks he's scored a wonder try,
He's feelin' mighty fine.
Except he's put the ball down on
The Leythers ten yard line!

Leigh v Wigan October 1973 at Hilton Park and the turning point of the game as Leigh go on to win 15 – 2

Half A Lane Too Thin

When they built the Wigan Pool
They got the size all wrong.
It's said it wasn't wide enough
Nor 50 metres long.
Folk say it was a metre short
And half a lane too thin.
And so if drawn on the outside
You knew you'd never win.
For while the others swam freestyle,
You'd end up as that bloke.
The one all squashed in half a lane,
And forced to swim side stroke.

Memories of Wigan International Pool.

From Blue Stripes To Cherry Hoops

I still remember my first game
When I was only ten.
Wigan v Northwich in The Cup
At Springfield way back then.
I'd go and watch The Latics games
I'd stand there with my dad,
Cheering with all the Wigan fans,
Exciting for a lad.

With Peter Houghton, Tommy Gore
Both dangerous in attack.
With John Brown in the Wigan goal
Big safe hands at the back.
But sadly it came to an end
For one day we went down,
To watch us play a Walsall team
But thugs had come to town.

Their fans ran over, cross the pitch
To our side of the ground.
They stormed onto the terracing
Fights raging all around.
Amidst the kicks and punches
There stood my poor old dad.
Trying to shield me from the fists,
His arms around his lad.

The police ran in with batons raised
And pulled us from the fray.
I swapped blue stripes for cherry hoops
After that fateful day.
Coz I would go to Central Park
Watch rugby games instead,
Where punches thrown were on the pitch,
Not inches from your head.

I've been a rugby league fan ever since but I still keep an eye out for
The Latics score every Saturday.

River Caves Virgin

I couldn't hold on any longer,
I knew that I must go,
I left my dad on the terrace,
To find where the cave rivers flow.
So this was my rite of passage
Like would-be Indian braves.
I followed my nose and soon I found
The entrance to the caves.

I wandered into darkness
To the sounds of waterfalls.
Wading across a yellow lake,
Where cavemen faced the walls.
These men were veteran cavers,
And soon I did discover,
They'd go with beer in one hand,
A fag held in the other.

I found myself a little gap,
I just looked straight ahead.
"Don't draw attention to yourself"
Wise words my dad had said.
But now I couldn't seem to go,
I was brastin' when I entered.
The men are bound to turn and stare,
I wish I'd never ventured.

And was that the half time hooter?
I was quickly filled with fear,
For the caves would soon be flooded,
And I had no scuba gear.
But nature finally took its course,
On me coat I wiped my hands.
I splashed towards the sunlight,
To the fresh air and the fans.

The River Caves were situated behind the Popular Stand at Central Park. These were really bad toilets, especially for a child. Rugby League Correspondent Dave Hadfield when writing about the last days of Central Park wrote in The Independent "Its toilets, the notorious River Caves, are a disgrace bordering on a health hazard."

The Man With The Shiny Shoe

When I was just a little lad
We'd all play in Mesnes Park.
We'd race down to a statue there,
An old Wigan landmark.

A well-dressed bloke sat in a chai,r
A man from Wigan's past.
And he must have been important,
To have his figure cast.

I can't remember who he was,
But I knew what to do,
I'd shut my eyes and make a wish,
And rub his shiny shoe.

I don't know when or why this custom started. The end of one shoe was always shiny, unlike the rest of the statue. Mesnes Park is actually pronounced Mains Park.

A View From A Bridge

On match days down at Central Park,
Some fans would always be,
Stood cheering from the corner bridge,
Watching the game for free.
If you couldn't get a ticket,
Or simply short of brass,
It was an opportunity,
You really couldn't pass.
A great view of a Wigan game,
Without spending a pound,
As long as all the action was
At that end of the ground.

Fond memories of Central Park. The bridge was known as The DSS Stand. Picture from www.wigan.rlfans.com, photographer unknown.

Pie And Cloddin

We'd all turn up at Grandma's house,
The top of Acton Street.
Coz that's where on a Saturday
The Sharkeys liked to meet.
A party would be sent out while
The rest would sit and wait,
For them to come back with the pies
From Laces, Standishgate.
We'd all tuck into fresh baked pies
And lots of cups of tea.
No better way to spend the day
I think you would agree.
Then in the kitchen there would be
Much mixin', rollin', proddin',
As Gran would make a special treat
Of homemade buttered cloddin.

Memories of the 1970s at my Grandma Sharkeys. The room would be full of aunties, uncles, cousins and of course lots of pie and cloddin*

*Cloddin - rolled out pastry with added raisins that had been 'clod in' the oven to bake. Served warm with butter.

Challenge Cup Final Memories

April '94 was the date
Martin scored a try that was great
He smashed the Leeds' shield
Ran the length of the field
And scored after speeding past Tait

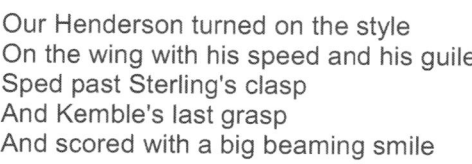

Our Henderson turned on the style
On the wing with his speed and his guile
Sped past Sterling's clasp
And Kemble's last grasp
And scored with a big beaming smile

Pie Crusts

Back in the 1970s
A perm was all the rage.
Young folk rushed down to hairdressers
And spent most of their wage.
But in Wigan it was different,
The stylists would despair,
Coz we all knew that eating crusts
Would give us curly hair.

My grandma and my mum would always get me tc eat my pie crusts
by saying "If you don't eat your crusts, you won't get curly hair."
As you can see in my school photograph, the curls were coming
along nicely. Photographer unknown.

Pies And Stout

Today's the day my Grandad
Would find his concertina.
We would be the audience
The back room his arena.

He'd squeeze and press the buttons
And play an Irish jig.
A song about O'Rafferty
Who had a naughty pig.

He'd mumble on for ages
To sounds of moans and curses,
Coz the song went on for forever,
With countless lines and verses.

But when he finally finished,
The pies would all come out.
And folk would toast Saint Patrick
With a glass of Irish stout.

Memories of my Grandad Sharkey on St. Patrick's Day

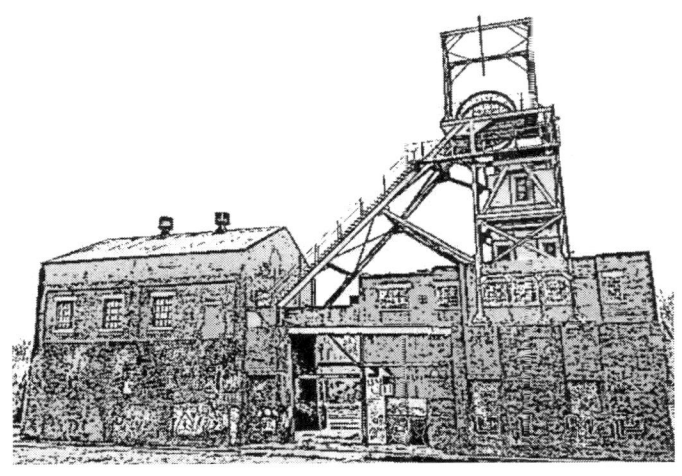

Three Miles Underground

When Wigan called on young John Clark
They found he wasn't home.
So talks they were conducted on
The pit head telephone.
For John was working down the mine,
And so when he was found,
An offer was relayed to him,
Some three miles underground.

The signing of John Clark from Castleford in 1965.

Star Wars Comes To Wigan

Making our way up Standishgate
A young me and my dad.
We're heading for the top of town,
I am a giddy lad.
We walk right up to Woolies,
Where we are promptly slowed.
A massive queue of folk are stood,
Snaking down Station Road.
Reluctantly we join the line,
There's nowt to do but stand.
The queue it doesn't move at all,
This wasn't what we planned.

It feels that we will never budge,
But at last we are there.
My dad he buys our tickets,
And we settle in a chair.
We're met by distant galaxies,
Where Jedis use the force,
To try and beat Darth Vader
And let good take its course.
I sit there in amazement,
I become an instant fan.
I lose myself and shout and cheer
For Leia, Luke and Han.

It's the 1970s and Star Wars fever grips Wigan. I remember waiting for ages outside in a long queue outside the ABC cinema with my dad for the next showing. It was well worth it.

Stamp On His Head, He Bleeds!

I've seen some people get worked up
When at a rugby game.
We all know it can get too much
Coz sometimes I'm the same.

I still recall a lass from Cas
Getting extremely mad.
Her veins were pumping in her neck
In front of me and Dad.

Increasingly frustrated with
Bad tackles and misdeeds.
She finally cracked and shouted out
"Stamp on his head, he bleeds!"

Wigan v Castleford, Central Park, circa 1990. Some fans need to calm down!

Grandma Sharkey's Secret

I want to share a secret
That came from Grandma Sharkey.
An Irish Cream to warm you up
When it is dark and parky.

Get yourself four free range eggs,
And condensed milk (large tin).
Camp coffee, four full tablespoons,
If the shops have got some in.

And now comes the naughty bit,
A pot of single cream,
And whiskey (half a bottle)
A cheap one, nowt supreme.

The ingredients are added,
One by one you mix them in,
Then you sample your creation,
And allow yourself a grin.

So now you know the secret,
Enjoy neat or with some ice.
A simple yummy Irish Cream,
For a fraction of the price.

Every Christmas I spend ages looking for the scrap of paper with this recipe on. I thought if it was in the form of a poem I wouldn't have the same problem finding it.

The Hand of G.O'D.

Do you recall the hand of God?
No not that Maradona,
No this lad fooled a rugby ref,
And did it good and proper.
It's Wigan, Saints at Central Park,
The scoreboard shows all square.
Lydon attempts to drop a goal,
Ball flying through the air.

O'Donnell tries to charge it down,
Hands stretching to the skies,
But still it sails between the posts
To win it for The Pies.
The Wigan fans they celebrate,
A sound of great elation,
But on the pitch, not all is right,
There is a remonstration.

Young Gus O'Donnell's going mad
He's pointing to his hand.
He says he touched the ball in flight,
The drop goal should not stand.
The flustered referee believes
That Gus is genuine.
He says the goal, it is does not count,
And Wigan do not win.

On replays of the incident
It all looks very clear.
His hand it does not touch the ball,
In fact it's nowhere near.
So boos for Gus O'Donnell,
The ref he sure did cod.
The Pies denied by a dodgy call,
And by the hand of G.O'D.

It's Good Friday, 1993 in front of a crowd of 29,839. Wigan have to settle for a draw in what was virtually a Championship decider at Central Park. Wigan still went on to win the title. Under today's rules the point would have counted. Ironically Gus was a Wigan lad and a former Wigan player. 'To cod' is local slang meaning 'to fool'.

Humble Pie

You'd all be forgiven for thinking,
It's due to our love of the pie,
They call us pie eaters in Wigan,
But that's not the full reason why.
We all love our meat and potato,
We eat lots of pie it's a fact.
But the story behind our nickname,
Comes from a cruel, despicable act.

A long time ago it did happen,
Nineteen hundred and twenty six,
When the folk of Wigan were miners,
And they chose to put down their picks.
Coz wages and safety were dire,
The union men were appalled,
So to try to improve the conditions,
A strike of all workers was called.

The country it came to a standstill,
As workers came out in support,
At the steelworks and at the railways,
And dockers who worked in the port.
But the colliery owners of Wigan,
They were heartless, cunning and sly,
And they starved all their men back to work,
And made them all eat humble pie.

So in Wigan the strike it was broken,
Men forced down the pits once again,
Working more hours but earning less pay,
For a life of misery and pain.
The miners of Wigan defeated,
Abused by greedy brow beaters.
No longer a town of strong and proud folk,
But a town of humble pie eaters.

Sometimes the truth can be painful. I prefer the theory that we're called pie eaters due to our love of pies.

Super Kel

Wigan v Fev at Central Park
A bad tempered affair.
When Kelvin became Super Kel
And soared into the air.
He missed the goal line mêlée,
Flew right over the top.
And smashed into the referee,
A super hero prop.

Wigan v Featherstone, Challenge Cup Quarter Final, Central Park 1994.

I went to this game with my wife-to-be who is a Fev fan. Needless to say we stood at opposite ends of the ground. Kelvin ran in from some distance and jumped over the top of a brawl and caught the ref squarely on the jaw. He later claimed that he was just peace-making.

Blue Monday

Today it is Blue Monday
According to the news.
The day that we are most depressed,
The day we get the blues.
So I grab myself some mint balls
From my old mint ball tin.
Get in the car and head to work
Where I can't help but grin.
I'm stared at by my colleagues
Who sigh and sulk and frown.
They don't know why I'm all aglow
While they are feeling down.
So I throw them all a mint ball
And tell them to enjoy,
And watch the transformation to
A room of smiles and joy.

Spread a little happiness. Give them an Uncle Joe Mint Ball. Wigan's finest.

Rugby League Family

I still remember Central Park,
The banter, jokes, the smart remark.
The rugby talk with fellow Pies,
The chants, the songs, the shouts, the tries.
But off I went to distant lands,
And said farewell to all the fans.

I've missed the craic for two decades,
But banter's back and back in spades.
Coz now with Twitter on my phone,
No more am I a Pie alone.
No more am I out in the cold,
I have returned back to the fold.

Who will we sign? The latest news.
Share my thoughts and game reviews.
So what went right and what went wrong?
Who's off form and who's on song?
Can we beat the opposition?
Can we gain that pole position?

We've got this game, it's in the bag.
Has Barry Chuckle got the flag?
We need to put up better kicks,
And can this ref count up to six?
Sharing the ups, sharing the downs,
The smiles, the tears, the laughs, the frowns.

And tweeting with the rival fans,
It's just like banter in the stands.
Bulldog, Rhino, Saint or Bull,
From Warrington, Leigh, Wakey, Hull,
To Barrow, Salford, Fev, Bramley.
We are the Rugby League Family.

Thanks to Twitter, I now exchange views and banter with like-minded rugby league fans, all who have a passion for the greatest game.

Polite Applause And Forced Smiles

The Rugby Football Union
The Wigan Club they asked,
To play a sevens tournament,
Forget about the past.
Twickers was full of rugger fans
Wanting our lads to fall,
But Wigan showed a masterclass
Of running with the ball.

Game after game they wooed the crowds
Despite the different rules.
With strength and fitness and top skills
They were nobody's fools.
They made it to the final where
The Wasps were swatted down.
The Mighty Pies victorious
They took the sevens crown.

Polite applause and forced smiles from
The old school tie brigade.
As Wigan held the cup aloft
The other teams outplayed.
The suited men of Union
All hung their heads in shame.
The Pies had come, turned on the style
Beat them at their own game.

Despite objections from RU bosses, Middlesex member Derek Mann invited Wigan to the Middlesex Rugby Union Sevens Tournament at Twickenham. It turned the event into a box office hit as on 11th May 1996, 60,000 spectators came to see how the RL lads would contend with the now professional RU players. They didn't do too bad beating Wasps 38-15 in the final.

Over To Our North Of England Correspondent

I always feel quite patronised,
A little bit despondent,
That the Beeb they feel the need
For A Northern Correspondent.
Are we a distant colony,
A strange and lawless land,
Who need specially trained reporters
To help you understand?
Where's the Southern Correspondent?
Why, there isn't such a bloke.
It must be classed as civilised
By The Beeb and other folk.

News readers hand over to The North Of England Correspondent in the same manner as they would The Middle East Correspondent. Are journalists given specialised BBC training in order to report the news from The North? Why no South Of England Correspondent?

Unbelievable

Some say that Neil Armstrong
Never reached the moon.
And some say Illuminati
Will be in power soon.
Some say that Elvis isn't dead
He's happy, fit and well.
Some say a flying saucer crashed
And landed in Roswell.
Some say that Billy Shakespeare
Didn't write them plays.
Some say it was the C.I.A.
That killed poor J.F.K.
Some say that Armageddon's here
Our time on Earth is up.
And some say that Sheffield Eagles
Did beat Wigan in the cup!

It's May 1998 and it's a big upset as the Sheffield Eagles beat Wigan in the Challenge Cup Final at Wembley. I have since convinced myself that this didn't really happened.

Central Park Players

You're half way through the book. Make yourself a nice cup of tea and grab a pencil.

Across

    1 Up, up, up and away!
       The Superman forward flew over the fray.

    4 At catching high balls he was simply supreme.
       Was it all that time spent on his trampoline?

    6 This player showed Tallis just how you should punch.
       Now he's found on the telly with the Sky bunch.

    7 A big Aussie giant with the name of a lass.
       With men on his back he would still make the pass.

    8 A "Butch" Wigan forward so blond and so bold.
       A tackling machine who left Morley out cold.

    9 When this fella scored, he'd celebrate in style.
       A wiggle of the hips and big beaming smile.

Down

    2 So quick off the mark, a try was soon his.
       For no one could catch this Mr. Whizz.

    3 Known as The Pearl, not ginger but black.
       He was revered by all in defence and attack.

    5 This 007 was licensed to score.
       His dazzling runs left the crowd wanting more.

    8 Another great player from Wigan St. Pats.
       Now sending us sleepy with too many stats.

Some of my favourite players I used to go and watch at Central Park.

(Answers on page 117)

Banished To Leigh

A Wigan boy comes down the stairs, he's looking pale and scared.
He sees his father in the room, decides to have a word.
"I have a small confession Dad, you'd better take a chair.
I just can't keep it in no more, I think it's time to share."

The father sits down on the couch, and looks up at his son.
He smiles and tries to look relaxed, and guess what is to come.
"Are you hooked on drugs my lad? Or do you think you're gay?
I'll love you just the same you know, no matter what you say."

His son now filled with confidence, begins to let it out,
As tears roll down his ruddy cheeks, he starts to rant and shout.
"I'm fed up with deceptions Dad, the false smiles and the lies!
What can I say, I know it's wrong, I SIMPLY DON'T LIKE PIES!"

The father stares back at his son, with anger in his eyes.
For 18 years he's brought him up, on meat n tater pies.
"Get out my house, you bring me shame, you are no son of mine!
And if I don't see you no more, well that will suit me fine!"

The son he knows he's gone too far, and tries to compromise.
He knows being a Wigan bloke, you must eat tater pies.
"But it's the crust that I don't like, I'm happy with the filling,
I gladly eat just meat n spuds, and stay if you are willing."

The father slumps in disarray, he's saddened and distraught.
The situation with his son, is worse than he first thought.
"What you've described is lobby lad, this simply cannot be.
Go find your stuff, get on your way, I banish you to Leigh!"

Pie and Lobby. It's a Wigan/Leigh thing.

The Impossible

The world has gone completely mad,
Pigs out my windows fly,
Towards the morning Western sun,
That's rising in the sky.
And hell has frozen over,
Summer snowflakes turning red.
The summer cuckoo can be heard,
And chicks have wet the bed.
This month's a month of Sundays,
With two Thursdays every week,
And all the hens are smiling,
White teeth inside their beak.
The Broomstick leaves are open,
Crows fly upon their back,
Grapes ripen on the willow,
And now the heron's black.
And Latics are at Wembley,
Full time is nearly up.
They score a last gasp winner,
And lift the FA Cup.

This was written after watching the impossible. It's May 2013 and Wigan Athletic have just beaten Manchester City to win the FA Cup. The poem refers to 'it will never happen' expressions from various countries.

Wigan: 1 Town, 2 Teams, 3 Trophies

In the Wigan trophy room
They're in a spot of trouble.
Latics have won the FA Cup,
The Warriors, the double.
They need a brand new cabinet,
Can anyone install?
The current one will just not do,
It's really far too small.

Who would have thought that in 2013, Wigan would be the centre of the sporting universe?

Curse Of The Wigan Shirts

Since their move to Langtree Park
It's gone from bad to worse.
Coaches sacked and injuries,
It's said there is a curse.
No exciting derby games,
The clashes are so boring.
Easy wins against The Saints
No longer so alluring.
So should I go and find my spade,
Dig up the centre spot,
And excavate the Wigan shirts?
You're joking, I think not.

Recalling the myth that Langtree Park has been cursed by the burying of Wigan shirts under the pitch by Wigan supporting builders. True or not it seems to have worked, the Saints haven't made the best of starts at their new stadium.

Blake Green

Blake Green was running red hot
Despite a nasty cheap shot
With only one eye
He scored a great try
And man of the match he got

Written after the 2013 Grand Final. Despite being hit in the second minute, while tackled on the floor, Blake, with one eye closed, guided Wigan to victory and won The Harry Sunderland trophy.

No Pies Are Left In This Vehicle Overnight

The people of Wigan are happy,
That crime is on its way down,
After a spate of daring thefts
Had blackened the name of the town.

The Chief he was ready for questions
As to how he'd managed this feat.
Had he used more surveillance?
Or paid for more police on the beat?

The Chief was under great pressure,
The critics were ready to pounce,
Had he spent over the budget?
The Chief he just grinned and announced.

"No need to pay for more Bobbies,
The answer was cheaper by far,
We just asked the good folk of Wiggin
To stick this in the back of their car."

I have this sticker on display in my car, although there's not much pie theft where I live in Yorkshire.

Three Stars

We deserve to have three stars
On our shirt for all to see.
Manly, Penrith, Brisbane,
I think would all agree.
A reminder of our past,
When taking up the fight.
A sign of what it means to wear
The cherry and the white.
An inspiration to the lads,
But importantly what's more,
Providing motivation,
To turn three stars into four.

Written back in 2013 after Widnes included a World Club Champion gold star on their regular kit. I'm pleased to say I few years later our WCC stars were incorporated as part of our club badge and we did gain a 4th star. Design by Jonny Ashton @JonnyAshy. Used with permission.

Four Gold Stars

The hooter sounds, the fans go wild
With scarves and flags unfurled.
The team has done it once again,
The best club in the World.
The players grin, champagne is sprayed,
The trophy's held up high.
I'm in a state of ecstasy,
I even drop my pie.

This generation's done us proud
I think you will agree.
They've written their own piece
Of Wigan Rugby history.
So well done lads for now we've done
What no club's done before.
No longer three gold World Club stars,
We proudly now have four.

Written in February 2017 after watching Wigan beat Cronulla at The DW Stadium to win their fourth World Club Challenge.

Russian Spies

There's Russian spy planes way up there,
Above the lands of Lancashire.
What have they seen? What have they viewed?
What do they want? Is it our food?
Have all those Russians had enough
Of caviar and stroganoff?
With high tech cameras in the skies
They're looking for our stocks of pies.
They're after hot pot recipes,
And how to make the best black peas.
They're on alert, searching for signs,
Of our secret jam butty mines.
And buried lakes of fine pea wet.
Our black puddings they must not get.
So at their cameras flick the V's,
Just smile and say "Lancashire cheese!"

It's May 2015 and a Russian spy plane is spotted over Lancashire.

Billy

So sixty years
Ago today,
Saw Mr Billy
Boston play,
His debut for
The Mighty Pies,
He scored the first
Of many tries.
He left his home
In Tiger Bay,
And to The North
He made his way.
A big man with
Great turn of speed,
Off down the wing
He would stampede.
With great side step
And strong hand off,
To Bill, the fans
Their caps did doff.
With Eric Ashton
Just inside,
Through tough defences
He would glide.
A record haul
Of tries he scored,
And in the town
He's still adored.
Not one to boast
About his fame,
Truly a legend
Of our game.

This was written on the 60th anniversary of Billy's debut for Wigan against Barrow. He went on to score 478 tries in 483 appearances for the Wigan club, between 1953 – 1968. A true Wigan Rugby legend.

Pies, Mints And Rock n Roll

I'm playing down in London
With my all-time favourite band.
I'm gonna be a rock star,
On my trailer I'll demand,
Lots and lots of tater pies,
With pots of warm pea wet.
Freshly delivered from The North
By special Lear jet.

Forget your recreation drugs
I won't be needing those,
Being a lad from Wigan,
I'll be popping Uncle Joes.
I'm gonna have a crazy night
And play the rock star role.
For one night only it will be
Pies, mints and rock n roll!

Written after finding out that I was due to play with favourite band, The Men They Couldn't Hang, at The Shepherd's Bush Empire in London. The night didn't disappoint. Photographer unknown.

Confiscated Pies

It's game day down in Castleford,
The Tigers v The Pies.
I head towards the entrance,
The queue is quite a size.
I finally make it to the front,
A man puts up his hand.
He looks rather official in
A coat with I.D. band.
He looks inside my plastic bag,
But doesn't seem to care,
Much for my knuckle dusters,
My smoke grenade and flare.
He reaches to the bottom and
Imagine my surprise,
He licks his lips and confiscates
My meat n tater pies.

Written after attending a Cas v Wigan game. I saw the security man confiscate a girl's can of coke, yet Wigan fans still managed to get in with a red smoke grenade.

Topless Pies

It's that time of year again,
The time when people try
To be the champion of the world
And eat a load of pie.
Athletes come from far and wide
To Wigan, home of pies,
They've had intensive training
And they want to win the prize.
But now it has been sabotaged
By the health and safety lot,
"You can't eat pies with crust tops on
It makes them far too hot!"
They've spoilt it for the athletes
For pie eating is their niche.
But a pie without a top on
Is not a pie, it's quiche.

It's December 2013 and controversy reigns at the annual World Pie Eating Championship in Wigan. You can't have pies without tops on!

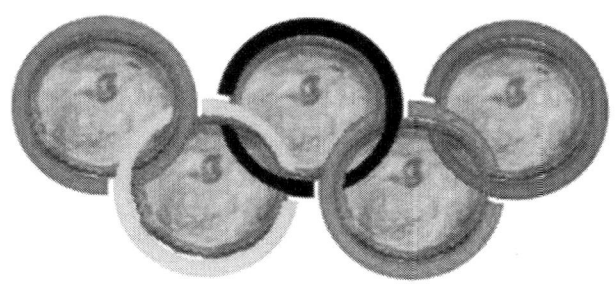

The Wrong Pies

It's that time of year again,
The time when people try,
To be the champion of the world,
And eat a load of pie.
And once again controversy
And much confusion reign,
Weeks of intensive training
All going down the drain.
The chef has made a big mistake,
He's sent the wrong size pies,
They should have been 5 inch across,
But these are twice the size.
So all results are null and void,
But still I don't know why?
If there's one thing that I've learnt in life,
You can't have too much pie.

Controversy continues at the 2014 World Pie Eating Championships.

Mint Ball Addict

My son he is addicted
To Uncle Joe's Mint Balls,
Coz without his daily fix
He suffers bad withdrawals.

I've caught him in the kitchen,
His hand stuck in the jar.
I've found discarded wrappers
On the backseat of my car.

I dread to think what he will do
If his addiction grows.
Smash em up in powder lines
And snort them up his nose?

The mint ball jar is soon emptied these days. I've had to start hiding it under my bed.

Wagin Bere Fetsvial Peom

Wolceme to ym peom
It's muldded and unlcaer
The letetrs rae all jubmled
And teh spllenigs seme qiute qeuer
Btu remmeber it wsa wrtiten
Wihle qufafing pnits of bere!

I always look forward to meeting up with my mate Danny Calderbank
at the Wagin Bere Fetsvial.

There's Only One True Derby Game

The first derby was a football match,
Or so the books all say.
A game with hundreds on each side
First played down Derby way.
But The 19th Earl of Derby
Did recently declare,
There's just two British sports events
His Derby name they bare.
The horse race down at Epsom was
The first they did endorse,
Where the then 12th Earl of Derby,
Did like to race his horse.
The other played between two teams
Whose rivalry is great.
Who play their rugby not far from
The Earl's Knowsley Estate.
To all you sports fanatics,
It may be a surprise,
There's only one true Derby game,
The Saints against The Pies.

Written on Good Friday 2015 before the 343rd Derby. True or false?
I'd like to think it's true.

Other sporting events linked to the Earls of Derby include:
The Stanley Cup (Canadian ice hockey) introduced by Lord Frederick Stanley the 16th Earl of Derby
The Lord Derby Cup (French Rugby League) introduced by Lord Edward Stanley the 17th Earl of Derby.

Heinz Roulette

Wigan is the home of Heinz, your beans all come from there
And I can still remember smells, of oxtail in the air
My mum worked at the factory, like many she was able
To buy us tins from factory shop, which came without a label

Instead there was a special code, ont tin t was embossed
And all these codes were on a list, but ours was often lost
So when it came to dinner time, the table would be set
And we would all settle down, for a game of Heinz Roulette

We had fifty seven options, so who would be the winner?
Beans on your toast or custard, for your Sunday dinner?
But no, a tin of peaches, and then a tin of meat
And being really hungry, we'd all tuck in and eat

Yes dinner time in Wigan, a time of taste sensations
All over town the kids would eat, strange food combinations
So if you see a gentleman, and gravy he is swiggin'
With a tin of prunes, don't fret, he's probably from W'iggin

Childhood memories. I still remember the code for beans had 'BV' in the middle of it.

Deconstructed Pie With Pea Jus

I'm in a swanky restaurant. The only Northern voice
The waiter's dressed in a posh suit. He asks me for my choice

A great big pon of lobby and some nice peawet will do

You mean a deconstructed pie with serving of pea jus

@PieEaterKev

Written after watching an episode of Masterchef

Beer And Tear Stains

It's England v The Green and Golds,
There's great anticipation.
Can we beat the men from Oz
And bring pride to the nation?
I've always watched these big games in
My Lions rugby shirt.
The stains of beer and tears on it
Tell of the years of hurt.
Is this the start of a new dawn?
I drink my beer and sigh,
Them Aussies have just run in yet
Another easy try.
And so there's disappointment
As we fail to win a-gain
When will we beat the Aussie team
And make them feel our pain?
Why do I get my hopes up for
It always ends in hurt?
A few more beer and tear stains
Have been added to my shirt.

Written after another loss to Australia in The Rugby League 4 Nations. After all these years, why do I get my hopes up? I should know better.

HAVE YOU EVER WONDERED HOW SANTA KEEPS RUDOLPH'S nose all aglow? ▶ HE LANDS HIS ◀ sleigh down IN WIGAN AND FEEDS HIM A QUICK Uncle Joe!

@PIEEATERKEV

Turkeys aren't nervous **IN WIGAN** THEY CAN ALL SLEEP SOUND IN THEIR BED COZ PEOPLE IN WIGAN *eat pies* WITH THEIR SPROUTS AT CHRISTMAS INSTEAD **@PIEEATERKEV**

I Only Have Pies For You

No pies for all those models
Found in a magazine.
None for all them actresses
Seen on my tv screen.
No pies for all them divas
You find singing the blues.
No pies for all them women
Who read the Sky Sports News.
My pies are for the lady
For whom my love is true.
So that is why, darling I
Only have pies for you.

A romantic Wigan poem.

We Make Pies Not War

There's bomb squad vans, exclusion zones,
Armed police make an appeal,
To stay away from Wigan Lane,
It all seems so surreal.
ISIS have come to Wigan town
Of that there is no doubt.
Pure evil's spread to Lancashire,
It's time to weed it out.
The police they swoop and grab their man
And force him to the ground.
He's overwhelmed and led away
His hands they have been bound.
So get into the police van lad
And don't come back no more.
Coz in our town I think you'll find,
We make pies not war!

Written in the aftermath of the Manchester Arena bombing. A suspect ISIS terrorist is arrested in Upper Dicconson St, Wigan and 'suspicious items' are found in a house off Wigan Lane. Unreal.

Who Needs Crusts?

When I was just a little lad
My mum would often say,
"Eat up your crusts, they make you strong
And help you on your way".
A fact not lost in Wigan town
With our pie love affair,
It's why our rugby team does well
And wins much silverware.
Unlike them folk over in Leigh
Who only eat pie fillin',
To stick it all inside a crust
They simply are not willin'.
And so it is in disbelief
I sit and rub my eyes.
A lobby gobbling rugby team
Has gone and beat The Pies!

It's June 2017 and after a wait of 33 years, the Leythers finally beat Wigan in a competitive game 50 - 34. This was written for life long Leigh supporter Damian "Who Needs Crusts?" Worden.

Pie Eyed

"I'm just off to the pie shop,
I'll only have the one."
But you know what us blokes are like,
Don't want to be outdone.
Coz waiting at the counter
Are my pie eating mates,
All tucking into large pork pies,
Pea chasers on their plates.
We down three meat n tater,
And then two chunky steak.
On my way home, a pie kebab,
That was a big mistake.
My wife's sat at the table,
Not happy that I'm late.
Coz I can't face the beer she's made,
She really is irate.
"You've had more than a swift one,
It's obvious you've lied.
You've had too many crusts again,
You're totally pie eyed!"

The term 'pie eyed' got me thinking. What if blokes nipped out for a quick Sunday pie while their wives made beer at home?

New Kit Revealed

Another Wigan lad is down
They've had to stop the play.
The physio is having yet
Another busy day.
The queue outside the treatment room
It just goes on and on.
The management at Wigan know
That something must be done.
Top specialists in kit design
Have flown from overseas,
To come up with solutions that
Will stop the injuries.
After intensive trials and tests
They have a new design,
That will protect the muscle groups,
The tendons, joints and spine.
So goodbye to torn ligaments,
Farewell to bones that snap,
Coz now the new kit is a roll
Of plastic bubble wrap.

Written during the 2017 season. A year that has seen the Wigan team decimated by injuries.

A New Anthem For England

As England face The Kiwis
There's great anticipation,
It's time to sing our anthem
A new one for the nation.
The Kiwis sing their anthem first,
Take up their Haka stance.
The English lads stand in a line
And throw a steely glance.
The Kiwis finish slapping thighs
And sticking out their tongue,
The time has come, there is a hush,
Our anthem's to be sung.
The English form a huddle tight,
Kiwis in disbelief,
As our lads break in flowered hats,
Knee bells and handkerchief.
And as the band begins to play
Our lads hop, skip and prance,
The crowd all stand with hand on heart
And sing The Floral Dance.

Written after calls for a new anthem to be sung at England sporting events.

Wot No Pie?

I went in hospitality
Down at the Wigan club.
I watched the game from the best seats
And had some reet posh grub.
And yes I guess it was quite nice,
All dressed in shirt and tie.
But still I missed my South Stand seat
And meat n tater pie.

Had a nice three course meal with my mate Kev Hill, but where was the pie? Photographer unknown.

Suck On An Uncle Joe

When David went to Elah to give Goliath grief,
It's said he had an Uncle Joe wedged right between his teeth.
He sucked upon that minty ball, till he felt all aglow,
Then spat it in his sling shot, took aim, and let it go.

The Patron Saint of England's known for bravery and honour,
But that is not the reason why he didn't end a goner.
When St George faced that scaly beast, not many people know,
The Saint's breath quenched that dragon's flames, for he'd sucked an Uncle Joe.

Robin Of Loxley dressed in green, in Sherwood he did roam.
With bow and arrow by his side, his fighting skills he'd hone,
But when he split that arrow shaft, before he drew his bow,
His merry mate, Big Friar Tuck, slipped him an Uncle Joe.

You've heard of them Red Indian tribes, their fights with General Custer,
Well they all summoned extra help, before they did all muster.
That Crazy Horse sat on the ground, and on his pipe did blow.
Before that battle at Big Horn, he smoked an Uncle Joe.

So if you need some extra help, if life's getting you down,
Then pop over to Lancashire, and to a Northern town.
Where they make sweets with magic powers, that keep you all aglow,
Unwrap the mint of legends and suck on an Uncle Joe.

Written while coughing in bed at 3am surrounded by Uncle Joe Mint Ball wrappers.

Dom Manfredi

Three cheers to Dom Manfredi
Despite a bad wound to his head he
Went in for two tries
Won it for The Pies
After two seasons out he was ready

Grand Final 2018 Wigan v Warrington.
After two years out with injuries and with his head stitched up,
Dom had a fantastic game in defence and attack.

Soggy

Soggy ticket, soggy hair,
Soggy shirt and underwear.
Soggy raincoat, soggy socks,
Soggy trousers, soggy Docs.
Soggy linesmen, soggy ball,
Soggy fans don't like that call.
Soggy toilets, soggy wee,
Soggy half time cup of tea.
Soggy programme, soggy readers,
Soggy Wigan cheerleaders.
Soggy whistle, soggy kicks,
Soggy drop outs neath the sticks.
Soggy tackle, soggy pass,
Soggy face rubbed in the grass.
Soggy burger, soggy pie,
Soggy Wigan winning try.
Soggy hooter, soggy cheers,
Soggy celebration beers.

Written after getting absolutely soaked while walking to and from The DW Stadium one August afternoon. Welcome to Summer rugby.

Wigan Yorkshire Dwarves

What's with this Northern Warrior?
All this Brigantes talk?
A tribe centred in Yorkshire,
Somewhere just North of York.
"And just like all us Wigan folk,
They had deep steely eyes."
I think someone's had too much beer
With their chips and pies.
He looks more like a Tolkien Dwarf,
Who lived in caves and pits.
So what's he doing on our badge,
On merchandise and kits?
A nod to our long history,
Some aspect from our crest,
Maybe the castle and the crown,
Would surely have been best.
But I'm not gonna get upset,
And get into a tizz.
I can't change my allegiance so
Wigan Yorkshire Dwarves it is.

Controversy as Wigan Rugby change their badge to a Brigantes Warrior. I guess I'll just have to get used to it. Up The Dwarves!

Have The Leythers Gone All Posh?

I've just seen a Ringtons van,
That's them that sell posh tea.
So why is it driving around
The dark back streets of Leigh?

Have The Leythers gone all posh?
Have they started to spend
Their money on the finer things,
Like Ringtons Special Blend?

Do they wash their lobby down
With fine loose leaf Earl Grey?
I have to say I never thought
That I would see the day.

Then it starts to make some sense
The van comes to a stop.
A lad holding an old sat nav,
Out of the van does hop.

"Is this Leigh, near Tonbridge, Kent?"
I say "I'm sorry son.
No this is Leigh in Lancashire
You've come to the wrong one."

I commented on Twitter that a Ringtons Tea van had passed my house so my area must be posh. Leyther @Dam64Worden challenged me to write a poem about a lost Ringtons van in Leigh.

Super Shiny Shoe

I really hope Sir Francis Powell
Had nothing bad to hide.
I pray he was a reet good lad
Before he went and died.
I hope he didn't get involved
In stuff unsavoury.
I hope he was a righteous bloke
In his community.

Coz if he was a naughty chap,
His statue may come down.
The one that stands in Wigan Park,
Just on the edge of town.
And children will cry floods of tears,
Their wishes won't come true.
For there'll be no more rubbing of
His super shiny shoe.

Written after Black Lives Matter supporters pull down a statute of slave trader Edward Colston in Bristol. This led to calls for other statutes to be removed while others were vandalised. Councils started moving statutes with a questionable history.

Enjoy A Pie Barm/Bap/Bun....

Bread cake, barm cake, stotty, barm,
Softie, morning roll.
Are just some names we call our bread
In a recent twitter poll.
Oven bottom, bara, bun,
Cob, batch, roll and bap,
Are also terms that people use
In places on our map.
While teacakes, muffins, scufflers,
Conclude this long bread list.
There may be loads of other names
Which have been simply missed.
But no matter what you say,
One thing's beyond debate.
If you shove a pie in one,
You'll find that it tastes great.
So if you come to Wigan Town,
Please make sure that you grab
A pie in what we call a barm,
A top Wigan Kebab.

Amazing how many names we have for bread.

Martial Arts Of Wigan

So purrin', parrin', porrin'
No matter what its name,
In alleyways of Wigan town
This 'sport' was much the same.
Men with clogs upon their feet
And stripped bare to their skins,
Would start fighting with each other,
By kicking at the shins.
Favoured by the colliers
To settle a dispute,
But if the local bobby came
They'd quickly stop and scoot.
And bets were also common,
The crowd they often would
Put money on the first to quit,
Or who would first draw blood.
The fights they could turn nasty,
In records it is said
Of people strangled on the floor,
And kicked hard in the head.
What happened to this fighting,
This Wigan martial art?
All faded with the mists of time,
Gone, never to restart?
Why take a walk down King St,
Just as the clubs all close,
But men now fight with fists, not clogs.
At least they all wear clothes!

Written after seeing an advert for a clog fighting exhibition at Wigan Museum. Family rumour has it my Great Grandad Fitzpatrick was part of the porrin' scene although we don't know if his role was fighting or betting.

Who Would Be A Referee?

That must 'ave been obstruction.
He never played it right.
That was a mile forward ref,
It wasn't even tight.
And surely that's a knock on?
That try should be denied.
You've gotta take em back the ten,
And gerrum all onside.
He nearly took his head off.
They stripped it two on one.
The lad was tackled in the air,
Trying to catch that bomb.
You don't know what you're doing,
It's plain for all to see.
So how much did they bribe you then,
You dodgy referee?
Surely that's a penalty,
The tackle was complete.
Why don't you just give them a try,
You are a bloody cheat!

Phrases often heard on the terraces and in the stands at Rugby League grounds, and these are the ones without expletives. Who would be a rugby referee?

Wigan Budgie Smugglers

Folk in the Wigan Rugby shop
Have had to tweak their range,
Coz due to global warming
It's time to make a change.
It's out with scarves and woolly hats
And in with 'Pie Beachwear,'
To wear upon the terraces
Under the Sun's hot glare.

Now Wigan vests and sun hats
Are the order of the day.
There's flip flops and bikinis,
And Warrior sun spray.
So now you'll find me at the ground
Cheering The Pies along,
In me Wigan budgie smugglers,
And cherry white sarong.

Written as a poem challenge from Wigan supporter @JaneMiller18 after a bit of banter on Twitter. I do love my Twitter poem challenges.

Joe Daniels

That Covid had arrived again,
Coughs, sniffles, feeling hot.
I kept taking paracetamol
But it failed to hit the spot.
In the middle of a sneezing fit
I remembered Mum and Dad,
Talking about a remedy
They took when they felt bad.
And so I poured some whiskey out,
Plopped in a Joe's mint ball.
I left it to infuse a while
Then in hope, drank it all.
Next morning the sore throat had eased,
I felt more on the up.
So when you're feeling out of sorts,
Joe Daniels you should sup.

A Wigan remedy. I even remember reading it as a recommendation in the Doctors weekly column in The Wigan Observer newspaper.

Scholeshenge

It's a Wigan winter solstice,
The Piegans start to meet,
Ont former site of Central Park,
To walk up Greenhough Street.

All dressed in robes, cherry n white
They climb up to Scholeshenge.
Time to appease them Rugby Gods,
Grand Finals to avenge.

There's offerings of tater pies,
And Uncle Joe's mint balls,
While ukulele banjos cue
The ancient chants and calls.

They hope the Gods are satisfied
With all this Wigan fayre,
And look forward to a season
With lots of silverware.

I always pass 'Scholeshenge' when driving into Wigan to visit my mum and dad.

Just A Bus Stop In Wigan

Since Beeching closed the stations
Poor Leigh has been without,
"Just a bus stop in Wigan!"
You hear Pie Eaters shout.
The Council have decided
That summat must be done,
"Cas and Dewsbury ave train stops,
And even Featherstone!"

And so a train is boarded,
(From Wigan Town of course),
They set off down to London,
A Northern tour de force.
They storm into The Commons,
Head for the gallery,
Throw corned beef, spuds and onions
That land on each MP.

The PM isn't happy,
There's tater in his eye,
"What do you think you're doing?"
The Leythers then reply.
"We want to ave a station,
And so we ave been sent,
By all our constituents
To lobby Parliament!"

Leigh is still one of the largest towns in Britian without a railway station. A victim of the Beeching cuts in the early sixties.

British Pie Week

On Monday I'll have butter,
Tuesday, chunky steak,
Wednesday, mince and onion,
The next day I will bake,
A great big meat n tater,
On Friday cheese and leek,
Yes it can only mean one thing,
It has to be Pie Week!

Every March Britain celebrates British Pie Week. That's just an average week in Wigan!

4th Of July

Let's set off lots of fireworks,
Come on and celebrate.
Forget those loud Americans,
Why should that lot dictate?
This day is so significant,
But not for independence.
This day's important to the folk
Who have Wigan descendants.
Because in 1954,
The date, 4th of July,
Meat rationing came to an end,
And we could eat meat pie!

Fourteen years of rationing ended on the 4th of July 1954.
Restrictions on the sale and purchase of meat and bacon were finally lifted and meat pies were back on the menu.

Trouble Down At Wigan Zoo

There's trouble down at Wigan Zoo
A snake has broken free.
A worry as it only eats
Pies for its lunch and tea.

It's been described as 12 foot long
With stripes cherry and white.
And if you have a pie in hand
It's likely it will bite.

Pie shops have been alerted
To check for pies amiss.
And watch for scaly customers
With tendencies to hiss.

And if you have a midnight pie
Best leave the big light on,
For in the room there might just be
A pie loving python.

This would make a great horror film.

Turkey Dinner Incident

When coming back from Yorkshire
The team would have their fill,
But every time, the same old food,
A regulation grill.
Team captain Dougie Laughton
Was fed up more than most,
When spying on the chairman's plate,
A juicy turkey roast.

Before the chairman entered,
Young Dougie swapped his plate,
And quickly sat back in his chair
Before it was too late.
The chairman started eating,
But half way through he stopped,
This wasn't what he usually had,
His dinner had been swapped.

He stared at all the players,
Eyes stopped at Dougie's place,
In front of him a turkey roast,
A smile on Dougie's face.
The chairman wasn't happy,
And shook an angry fist,
And by next morning Doug was on
The Wigan transfer list.

The chairman wasn't joking,
And soon young Dougie found,
That he was leaving Central Park,
For Widnes he was bound.
So if you play for Wigan,
And you want to keep your post,
It's probably best that you don't eat
The chairman's turkey roast.

Dougie made 180 appearances for Wigan between 1967 - 73. He went on to have a successful career at Widnes and even captained his country before moving into coaching.

Sheep Stops Play

Little Bo Peep has lost her sheep
And doesn't know where to find them.
Well they've made their mark
At Central Park,
The police not far behind them.

Wigan v Broughton Rangers, Central Park, 1923
Play is interrupted while two police officers try to catch a sheep that has wandered onto the pitch. It is eventually caught by two Welsh lads playing for Wigan.

Pie-rish

The Fitzpatricks and The Sharkeys
They crossed the Irish Sea
And put down roots in Wigan Town
In the 19th Century
Am I Irish, am I English?
A harp or rose of red?
I need a new identity
So I've made one up instead
And so on application forms
My details I fill in
For ethnic status, I write down
"Of Pie-rish Origin"

I Don't Wanna Talk About it

I don't wanna talk about it,
How we wouldn't let them pass.
Wave on wave of Saints attack,
But our defence was class.
I don't wanna talk about it,
But we threw the ball out wide,
And finally scored a well worked try,
We looked the stronger side.
I don't wanna talk about it,
How that tackle wasn't high,
It gave the Saints a way back in,
The game was now a tie.
I don't wanna talk about it,
How that final hooter sounded,
The upright hit, that freaky bounce,
The Saints, the ball they grounded.
I don't wanna talk about it,
How hard it was to take,
The sense of total disbelief,
And subsequent heartache.
I don't wanna talk about it,
And the first person to say,
"Come on now Kev, it's just a game"
Will be sent on their way!

Written after losing The 2020 Grand Final in dramatic circumstances. The next morning my children were asking me what happened and who had won? I said I didn't want to talk about it but slowly proceeded to tell them over the course of the morning. I guess it was a kind of therapy.

Dr Kathleen Drew Baker (Mother Of The Sea)

Our Kath was in the kitchen,
Hot lobby in the pan,
When she was asked if she could help
The people of Japan.
For Kath had done some research,
On seaweed cultivation,
This research was much needed by
The poor war weary nation.
She said that she would love to help,
She wouldn't charge a fee,
But asked if they could kindly wait
Until she'd had her tea.
Her studies of the seaweed
That's used in lava bread,
Helped farmers in The Orient
Grow seaweed more widespread.
Now every year they celebrate
This clever lass from Leigh,
And in Japan she's known to all
As 'Mother of The Sea.'

To make sushi a special kind of seaweed, nori, is needed. However growing it is difficult & unpredictable. This meant that after the 2nd World War the Japanese nori industry went into decline. Such was the impact of Kath's research, in Japan she became known as the Mother of the Sea. Japanese nori farmers have an annual festival on 14th April known as Drew Day. Not bad for a lass from Leigh.

There's Always Time For Pie

At the start of all creation, there was Adam and Eve.
Who were joined by a big serpent, the Devil we believe.
But when he tried to tempt young Eve, she looked him in the eye.
"Your apple mate will have to wait, I'm still eating me pie."

When Moses led the Israelites, he stopped at the Red Sea.
Pursued by Pharaoh's army, he sat to eat his tea.
Although they urged him to make haste, or they would surely die.
Before parting them mighty waves, he chomped upon a pie.

And when the Good Samaritan, helped that bloke on the road.
By putting him back on his feet, in bandages he clothed.
He also found him shelter and subsidised the guy,
Advising him to treat his self, to peawet and a pie.

When five thousand had gathered out, to hear what Jesus said.
It's thought that he did feed them all, on two fish and five bread.
But the fish was smelling funny, the bread was really dry
He thought he'd like to treat them, so he conjured lots of pie.

The Bible, (Wigan Edition), is full of sound advice.
On how we all should live our lives, and stay away from vice.
It also tells us when we can, that we should always try,
To all enjoy life to the full. There's always time for p e.

Whatever your 'pie' is in life, make sure you allow plenty time for it.

Keeping The Faith

It had been five halves of play
Since we last scored a try,
The next game for The Warriors
Was gonna be close by.
I couldn't find a good excuse
To pass up on the game,
So off I went to Castleford,
Expecting much the same.

In with all the Wigan fans
I found myself a space,
Ready to watch another loss
I put on my brave face.
So imagine my delight
When we crossed for a try,
I was relieved we'd scored at last,
I cannot tell a lie.

But not content with just one try,
We scored another three,
And nilled The Tigers at their home,
A well earned victory.
And when the final hooter went,
The fans were on a high,
The lads were back to winning ways,
I was a happy Pie.

When your team is doing well,
Us fans are more inclined
To go and fill the terraces,
But I think you will find,
Watching your team take the pitch
When they don't have a shout,
Keeping the faith and see them win,
Is what it's all about.

An unexpected enjoyable afternoon in Castleford. However the 2021 season was generally one to forget.

A Season To Forget

This season hasn't been the best
I think you would agree.
I'd hide behind the sofa
When we were on TV.
I only made it to one game,
Ironically we won.
But watching our inept attack,
Was anything but fun.
For the fans sat in the stands,
Home games must have been torture.
I guess there are some benefits
Being exiled here in Yorkshire.

Here's to a better season next year. More pie offerings required at Scholeshenge to appease the Rugby Gods I think.

Smuggling Pies

The Tykes have risen and rebelled, they want a change of scene.
So it's Hail President Boycott, and farewell to The Queen.
They've had enough of other folk, the Tykes are staying put.
All goods are made in Yorkshire now, as trade links have been cut.

Towards the hills of Lancashire, a wary eye is cast,
By guards with large binoculars, on top of Emley Mast.
A mum and dad in Lancashire, they worry for their son.
He's stuck in Wakefield due to this, Yorkshire re-bell-ion.

Back in their house in Wigan town, they stock up with supplies,
And smuggle past the border guards, the finest Wigan pies.
They head back to the freelands but they stop off on the way.
They've arranged a little meeting, to make their journey pay.

They meet a Yorkshire dealer and inspect a case of goods,
For going back the other way, the finest Yorkshire puds.

Is the tower on Emley Moor just a transmitter? I'm not convinced. It's too wide to be just a mast. It think it's a lookout tower for when Yorkshire becomes a republic.

Wigan Casino

In Wigan they all loved to dance,
It weren't just pies and coal,
Coz in the 1970s,
It embraced Northern Soul.
The people travelled from afar,
They'd heard of Wigan's fame.
They all headed to a ballroom,
The Casino was its name.
They'd come and dance throughout the n ght
To Shep and Bobby Paris,
The Keys and Jimmy Radcliffe,
Tobi Legend and Dean Parrish.
But the council wanted office space,
I hope they harbour guilt,
Bulldozers came and knocked it down,
Yet nothing else was built.
And so it was in '81
The venue bid adieu,
To the sounds of Mr Wilson,
Love You, Indeed I do.
But Northern Soul it still lives on,
Casino tears now wept,
Coz Wigan folk are dancing still,
The faith it has been kept.

This was written to celebrate 40 years since the 1st Northern Soul All-nighter at Wigan Casino. Although I was too young to go to The Casino, I enjoy the music that is still played today.

A Pie A Day

The prices charged for energy
Are going through the roof.
I don't know how I'll pay for it,
I'm anxious, that's the truth.
There doesn't seem an answer
In any shape or form,
So I've thought of a solution,
I hope will keep me warm.
I'm gonna eat potato pies,
One every day so that,
When the winter comes around
I will be big and fat.
And with all that insulation,
I will not feel the chill,
No need to turn my boiler on,
And thus reduce my bill.

It's August 2022 and there's real concern as energy bills are set to rocket in winter. Politicians and economists don't seem to have an answer. I don't think they've thought of the pie solution.

Answers: Central Park Players

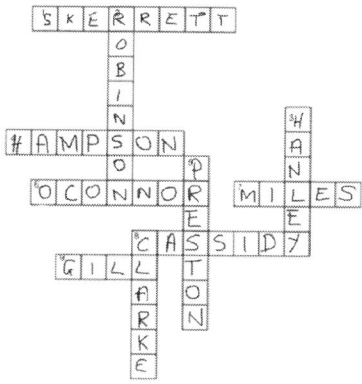

Also Available

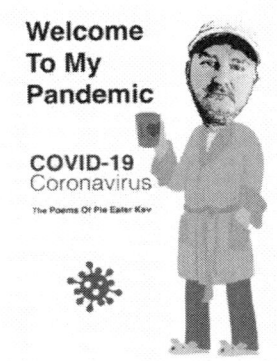

The debut book of poetry by Pie Eater Kev. Welcome To My Pandemic is a collection of poems written during The Covid Pandemic. A time of lockdowns, social distancing, face masks and rainbows. A time when a Scotch Egg was officially declared a substantial meal, and new words such as Blursday and Quaranteenager appeared. From light hearted verse to more personal and reflective poems, you're sure to enjoy this first offering from the Wigan Wordsmith. So strap yourselves in and get ready to ride The Coronacoaster.

Published May 2021

Also Available

There Once Was A
Fella From Wigan...

The Limericks of Pie Eater Kev

The second book of poetry from Pie Eater Kev. Following on from his international non best seller "Welcome To My Pandemic", this book celebrates that well-loved five line poem, The Limerick. A self-confessed limerick addict, The Wigan Wordsmith presents a collection of his own favourite verses. More comedic in nature than the traditional whimsical, nonsensical style limerick these poetic jokes were mostly written in the pub over a pint. Th s is an ideal book to dip in and out of, and it's sure to put a smile on your face. Who knows, you may even laugh.

Published November 2021

Printed in Great Britain
by Amazon